Contents

Wise Guy

For the LORD gives wisdom, and from his mouth come knowledge and understanding.

PROVERBS 2:6

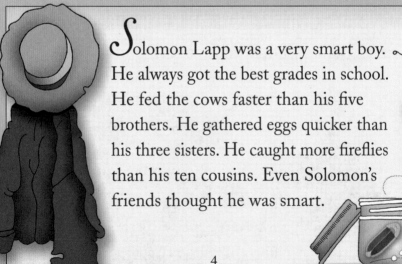

Solomon Lapp was a very smart boy. He always got the best grades in school. He fed the cows faster than his five brothers. He gathered eggs quicker than his three sisters. He caught more fireflies than his ten cousins. Even Solomon's friends thought he was smart.

4

The Wisdom of
Solomon

A Solomon Lapp and Friends Amish Storybook

WANDA E. BRUNSTETTER
Illustrated by Phil A. Smouse

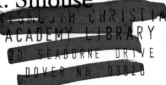

BARBOUR
PUBLISHING

To all my Amish friends and their
wonderful children and grandchildren.
W.E.B.

For the real Solomon Lapp
and his little brother Mervin
who gave me the idea in the first place.
P.A.S.

© 2009 by Wanda E. Brunstetter and Phil A. Smouse

ISBN 978-1-61626-701-8

All Pennsylvania Dutch words are taken from the *Revised Pennsylvania German Dictionary* found in Lancaster County, Pennsylvania.

All scripture quotations, unless otherwise indicated, are taken from
the HOLY BIBLE, NEW INTERNATIONAL VERSION®. NIV®. Copyright ©
1973, 1978, 1984 by International Bible Society. Used by permission of
Zondervan. All rights reserved.

Published by Barbour Publishing, Inc., P.O. Box 719, Uhrichsville,
Ohio 44683, www.barbourbooks.com

*Our mission is to publish and distribute inspirational products offering
exceptional value and biblical encouragement to the masses.*

Member of the
Evangelical Christian
Publishers Association

Printed in the United States of America.
Versa Press, Inc., East Peoria, IL 61611; May 2012; D10003297

One day a horse and buggy
pulled up to the big barn
behind Solomon's house.

Uncle Noah, a minister in the church,
climbed down from the buggy. He patted
Solomon's head and said, "Remember, it's the
Lord who gives wisdom. Before giving advice,
it's best to pray and ask God for wisdom."

"I'll remember," Solomon said with a nod.

Later that day, Solomon's friend
Willie King came by in his pony cart.

"I've got a problem. Since you're so *schmaert*
[smart], I hope you can help," Willie said when
he joined Solomon in the swing on his front porch.
Solomon smiled. "Please, tell me about it."

Willie rubbed his chin and puckered his brow. "I've been trying to teach my dog, Sam, some tricks. But Sam sits and begs when I say, 'Roll over.' And he rolls over on his back when I say, 'Sit!' Do you know what I can do?"

7

Solomon scratched the side of his head as he thought. "*Jah* [Yes], I know just what you can do!"

Solomon jumped up and ran into the yard. "When you want the dog to roll over, roll on the ground." Solomon dropped to the grass and rolled one way, and then another.

"When you want the dog to sit, do this."
Solomon put both feet together, squatted down,
and held his hands in front of his chest.

"*Danki* [Thanks], Solomon. I'll give it a try!"
Willie climbed into his pony cart and left for
home.

Solomon went to the barn to do his chores.

A few minutes later, he heard someone whistling. Solomon looked out the barn door and spotted his friend John Mast riding in on a scooter. John dropped the scooter to the ground and raced into the barn, waving his hands.

"I came because I need your advice," John said as he flopped onto a bale of straw.

Solomon took a seat beside his friend. "What's the problem?"

"One of our cows gets nervous when it's time to milk," said John. "She fusses and twitches her tail. What should I do?"

"Follow me!" Solomon led John into a stall where a black-and-white cow stood chewing its cud.

"If your cow gets nervous when it's time to milk, this is what you should do." Solomon grabbed the cow's tail and gave it a pull.

"Danki," John said with a nod.

As Solomon followed John out of the barn, he decided it felt good to be so smart. He was glad he could help two of his friends. In fact, Solomon felt so pleased with himself, he reached around and gave himself a pat on the back.

The next day, Willie came to see Solomon again.

"How did things go with your dog?" Solomon asked.

Willie frowned.

"When I rolled on the grass, the dog licked my face. When I sat up and begged, the dog brought me a bone!" Willie grunted. "You gave me bad advice."

Willie climbed into his pony cart and took off down the road, sending gravel flying in all directions.

Solomon flopped onto the grass with a moan. "Oh no! What could have gone wrong?"

Awhile later, John came wobbling down the lane on his scooter.

"How's your cow?" Solomon asked. "Is she calmer now?"

John shook his head. "When I pulled the cow's tail, she kicked me in the knee and sent my hat flying."

16

John limped back to his scooter and rode away, mumbling, "I'll never ask your advice again."

Solomon kicked a stone with the toe of his boot and headed for the house. "Maybe I need to think harder the next time someone wants my advice."

On Saturday, after Solomon's chores were done, he decided to play in the yard.

"Do you want to jump on the trampoline with me?" Solomon asked his sister Sara.

Sara nodded and gave Solomon a big grin. "Me first!" she shouted as she raced for the trampoline.

Solomon and Sara took turns jumping; then they jumped together.

Solomon stopped jumping when he saw his cousin Abe come into the yard. "Would you like to jump on our trampoline?" he called to Abe.

Abe shook his head. "I can't stay long. I came to ask you a question."

Solomon climbed off the trampoline, but
Sara kept jumping.

"What's your question?" Solomon asked Abe.

"I went to the dentist the other day, and he
said I'm not getting my teeth clean enough."
Abe opened his mouth really wide. "What do
you think I should do, Solomon?"

Solomon smiled. "I'll be right back!"
He raced into the house and
returned with a bar of soap.

"What's that for?" asked Abe.

"Whenever I don't get my hands clean
enough," said Solomon, "Mom tells me to use
more soap."

"Danki!" Abe took the soap and
headed for home.

On Sunday before church, Abe returned the bar of soap to Solomon.

"Keep your soap," he said with a grunt. "And keep your advice!"

"What happened?" Solomon asked. "Didn't the soap get your teeth clean?"

"It tasted awful." Abe frowned. "And thanks to your *dumm* [dumb] idea, I've been blowing bubbles all morning!"

During recess on Monday, Solomon was playing ball.

"I've got a problem," Becky Yoder called. "Can you help?"

"What's the problem?" asked Solomon.

"I have two cats that look alike. How can I tell them apart?"

Solomon tipped his straw hat and grinned. "That's easy. Put green paint on one of their tails!"

Becky smiled. "Danki, Solomon!"

"How are your cats?" Solomon asked Becky the next day.

She frowned. "I put green paint on one cat's tail, and—"

Just then, Uncle Noah showed up. The seat of his buggy was covered with green paint. So were Uncle Noah's pants!

"Remember Solomon," said Uncle Noah, "before giving advice, it's best to pray and ask God for wisdom."

Solomon suddenly understood why all of his advice had turned out bad. "I will, Uncle Noah! From now on, I will pray for God's wisdom before I give advice!"

Stuck iN the Mud

*Do not withhold good
from those who deserve it,
when it is in your power to act.*

PROVERBS 3:27

Sara's stomach rumbled and grumbled.

"I'm hungry," she said. "I wish I had something to eat."

Dad took a package of gum from his pocket and gave Sara a piece.

"*Danki* [Thanks]," said Sara.

Dad nodded and smiled. "Remember, God wants us to share with others."

That afternoon, Sara and her brother Mervin went shopping with Mom.

"Can I have some of your candy?" Mervin asked Sara as they left the store.

"No!" Sara took the lollipop from her mouth, and the candy slipped from her fingers.

Plop!—it fell in the dirt!

Mervin looked at Sara and said, "That wouldn't have happened if you had shared!"

When they got home from shopping, Mom gave everyone an apple.

Sara polished her apple with her apron and took a bite. "Yum!" Then she wandered outside and climbed on the fence.

Judy, their old buggy horse, plodded over to the fence and opened her big mouth really wide.

"You can't have my apple," said Sara.

Judy shook her head and bumped the
fence with her nose. The apple rolled
out of Sara's hand and dropped on the
ground. Judy scooped up the apple with
her great big teeth—*chomp, chomp, chomp!*

Sara ran to the house in tears.

That night after supper, Mom placed an apple pie on the table. She gave a piece to Dad and each of the children.

Sara smacked her lips. "I love *epplebei* [apple pie]!" She ate half her piece and said, "I'm full."

"I'll finish your piece," said Sara's sister Katie.

"No," said Sara. "You might get my germs."

"I don't mind a few germs," Katie replied. She reached across Sara, bumped the plate with her hand, and the pie went—*splat!*—on the floor!

Dad looked at Sara and said, "That wouldn't have happened if you had shared."

During recess the next day, Sara raced to the swing.

"Can I have a turn?" asked Sara's friend Emma.

Sara shook her head and spun the swing around.

When the school bell rang, Sara stumbled off the swing and fell on the ground.

"That wouldn't have happened if you had shared," Emma said as she helped Sara stand.

After school, Sara worked on a puzzle. "Can I help?" asked Sara's brother Clarence.

"No," said Sara, "you'll mix up the pieces."

"You're selfish," Clarence mumbled.

He bumped the puzzle box, and—*whoosh!*—all the pieces fell on the floor!

Solomon, who sat across from Sara, shook his head and said, "That wouldn't have happened if you had shared."

Little sister Barbara nudged Sara's
arm as she slumped in her chair. "I'm bored."

"Why don't you color a picture?" Sara
suggested.

Barbara raced out of the room and returned
with a coloring book and a box of crayons.

Sara frowned. "You can't use those. They're
mine!"

Barbara opened the box and took out
a crayon.

"Put that back!" Sarah shouted.

She grabbed the crayon and gave it a tug.
Barbara tugged back. *Crack!*—the crayon
snapped right in two!

"Now look what you've done!" Sara grabbed
the box of crayons and stomped out of the
room.

"We're having company today," Mom said the next morning, as she brushed Sara's hair and put it in a bun.

"Who's coming?" Sara wanted to know.

"Your cousins Annie and Abe." Mom handed Sara her doll. "Be sure to share your toys with your cousins and play the games they want to play."

Sara held her doll as she waited on the porch. Solomon, Clarence, and Mervin waited there, too.

Soon Annie and Abe rode in on their scooters.

"It's starting to rain," Solomon said. "Let's play in the barn."

Annie and Abe put their scooters on the porch. Then the children all ran to the barn.

"Let's pet the horses," Abe suggested.

"I don't want to," said Sara.

The boys scampered off to the horses' stalls, but Annie stayed with Sara.

"Let's play hide and seek," said Annie.

Sara shook her head. "I don't want to play that game. I'd rather play with my *bussli* [kitten]."

Sara tucked her doll under one arm
and climbed the ladder to the hayloft.

Annie followed.

Sara found her kitten lying
in some straw. She knelt on the
floor, set her doll aside, and
put the kitten in her lap.

Annie sat next to Sara.
"Can I pet the bussli?" she
asked. Sara shook her head.

Just then a mouse skittered across the floor.
The kitten leaped off Sara's lap and chased
after the mouse. Sara and Annie squealed and
jumped on a bale of hay.

"The rain's stopped,"
Solomon called from
below. "Let's go outside
now and play."

Sara picked up her doll. Then she and Annie climbed down the ladder.

Outside, the sun shone brightly, but there was water and mud puddles everywhere.

"Can I play with your doll?" Annie asked Sara.

"No," said Sara. "I'd rather not share."

"Pleeease," Annie pleaded. She grabbed the doll's arm and gave it a tug. Sara pulled on the doll's other arm.

Then Annie let go, and—*plop!*—Sara landed in a murky mud puddle! She tried to stand, but seemed to be stuck.

"I'm stuck in the mud," Sara cried. "I can't get up!"

Abe pointed at Sara and shook his head. "You sure look funny sitting there in the mud."

Annie giggled, while Solomon held his sides and laughed.

Tears rolled down Sara's cheeks. "It's not funny!"

Solomon's head bobbed up and down. "*Jah* [Yes], it sure is."

Solomon reached his hand out to Sara. "Here, let me help you," he said.

Solomon pulled, but Sara didn't budge.

Abe grabbed Solomon's other hand and he pulled, too.

Sara remained stuck in the mud.

Annie took Abe's hand and gave a sharp pull.

They all pulled and pulled and pulled.

Sara felt her body pull free just a bit.
She was almost on her feet when—*splat!*—
Solomon fell into the mud!

"Oops," he said, laughing and splashing
Sara with water. Sara laughed and splashed him
right back.

Soon Sara, Solomon, Abe, and Annie were
all laughing and splashing each other.

"I learned a good lesson today," Sara said when the splashing was done.

"What did you learn?" asked Solomon.

"I learned that it would have been better to share my doll than get stuck in the mud." Sara smiled at Annie. "From now on that's just what I'm going to do!"

Lazy Bones

*Laziness brings on deep sleep,
and the shiftless man goes hungry.*

PROVERBS 19:15

Solomon flopped on the grass
and propped his head in his hands.
He was supposed to do his chores
after school, but it felt so good
to lie in the yard looking up at the
clouds. Solomon's eyes grew heavy,
and he was almost asleep when
something brushed his cheek.

Solomon's nose twitched. His eyes
snapped open. Solomon's older brother,
Paul, tickled Solomon's nose with
a piece of straw.

"Wake up, *faul* [lazy] bones!"

Solomon grunted. "Go away!"

Paul pulled the straw down the side of
Solomon's face. "It's not good to be lazy.
It pleases God when we all do our work."

Solomon yawned as he scrambled to his feet.
Then he followed his brother to the barn.

Paul handed Solomon a broom. "You can
sweep the floor while I help Dad move
some hay."

Solomon frowned. "I don't like to work.
I'd much rather play."

Swish! Swish! Solomon swiped the broom across the floor and yawned. "This is so boring."

Dust and bits of straw flew up and tickled his nose. "Ah-a-a-choo!"

Solomon spotted the rope hanging from the beam overhead. "It sure would be fun to swing on that!"

Solomon set the broom aside and climbed the ladder to the hayloft. He grabbed the rope, put one foot on the knot, and pushed off. *Whoosh!* Solomon's breath caught in his throat as he sailed across the barn.

"Yippee! This sure is fun!"

"What do you think you're doing?"
Paul called from below.

"I'm swinging on the *schtrick* [rope],"
Solomon replied.

Paul shook his finger. "You're supposed to be
sweeping the floor, lazy bones."

Solomon dropped into a mound of hay and
picked up the broom. "I'd much rather play," he
mumbled.

"It's your job to feed and water the horses today," Dad told Solomon the following day.

Solomon knew better than to argue; but it was such a nice day, and he wanted to play.

With head down and shoulders slumped, he headed for the barn.

Ne-e-e! Ne-e-e! Mom's buggy horse, Judy, greeted Solomon as he stepped into her stall. She whinnied again and nuzzled his hand with her nose.

Solomon snickered. He loved to pet the horses. It was a lot more fun than feeding them!

Solomon gave Judy a bucket of oats, then he moved to the next horse's stall.

Meow! Meow! One of the barn cats rubbed Solomon's leg.

Solomon bent down and picked up the cat. "Do you want to play?"

Solomon found a ball of string and took a seat on a bale of straw. He put the cat on the floor and dangled the string in front of its nose.

Meow! Slap! Slap! The cat batted at the string and rolled on the floor.

"What are you doing?" asked Paul when he entered the barn again.

"I'm playing with the cat," Solomon said with a grin.

Paul frowned. "You're supposed to be feeding the horses."

Solomon shrugged. "I was, but I stopped to play."

"You'd better get back to work, or I'm going to tell Dad you're a lazy bones." Paul put the string back on the shelf.

With his head down and shoulders slumped, Solomon headed to the stall to feed the next horse.

"There's going to be a barn raising at Uncle Noah's today," Dad announced during breakfast the next day. "We will all go there to help."

Solomon frowned. "But it's Saturday, and I want to play."

Paul thumped Solomon's head. "You can play some other time, lazy bones."

Solomon grunted. "I'm too young to help build a barn."

"There will be jobs for everyone today," said Dad.

Sara rubbed her stomach and smacked her lips. "Think of all the good food we'll have to eat. Now that's something to look forward to!"

The horse pranced and the buggy bounced
as they headed down the road toward Uncle
Noah's. Solomon turned in his seat and stared
out the back of the buggy. The sky was blue,
and the sun shone bright. It was the perfect day
to run and play—but not a good day for work!

"Here we are," said Dad as he guided their
horse and buggy up Uncle Noah's driveway.
"Now let's all find a job to do!"

Solomon spotted his friends John and
Willie across the yard. He hopped down from
the buggy and ran to greet them.

"Let's do something fun," Solomon suggested.

Willie shook his head. "I thought we came here to work."

Solomon frowned. "I'd rather play."

John thumped Solomon on the back. "Maybe there will be time to play when the work is done."

Uncle Noah handed Solomon a hammer and a can of nails. "I'm glad you came to help out. Those who work hard will eat well today."

Solomon slipped on a pair of gloves and hammered awhile. *Bang! Bang! Bang!*

"Oh no!" he groaned. "I've nailed my glove to a piece of wood!"

Solomon dropped the hammer and shook his head. "I'm done with all this! Hammering *neggel* [nails] isn't fun at all!"

He glanced around to be sure no one was looking, then he hurried off to the creek. He flopped on the grass and removed his shoes. He wiggled his bare feet in the chilly water.

Solomon sat until his toes went numb. He heard laughter coming from the worksite.

Everyone must be having a good time, Solomon thought; but he felt lonely and bad that everyone else was helping while he had run away to play.

His stomach rumbled. *It must be almost time for lunch.*

"But if I have done no work, I don't deserve a share of the food. I must return and show them I am not a lazy bones."

Solomon slipped into his shoes and hurried back to the worksite.

"I'm ready to work!" he told Uncle Noah.

"I'm glad to hear it." Uncle Noah smiled and patted Solomon's head. "It's not good to be lazy. It pleases God when we all do our work!"

Sweet Sleep

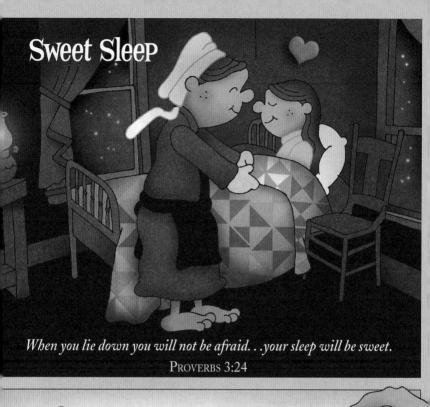

When you lie down you will not be afraid. . .your sleep will be sweet.
PROVERBS 3:24

Sara had just put on her nightgown when Mom stepped into the room.

"Are you ready for bed?"

Sara nodded. "I washed my face and brushed my teeth."

She climbed into bed. Mom covered Sara with a quilt and kissed her cheek.

"May your sleep be sweet," Mom whispered as she blew out the lantern by Sara's bed.

The door clicked shut. Sara closed her eyes and was almost asleep, when—*Whoosh! Whoosh!*—the wind whistled outside her window. Sara shivered and pulled the quilt over her head. She didn't like strange noises. She was afraid of the dark.

When Sara went downstairs to breakfast the next morning, she felt tired and grumpy. Her family all sat at the table—Mom, Dad, Solomon, Mervin, Clarence, Paul, Aaron, Owen, Barbara, Katie, and Carolyn. Sara yawned, flopped into a chair, and laid her head on the table.

"Are you feeling all right?" Mom asked.

Sara didn't want to admit that she'd heard strange noises and hadn't slept well because she'd been afraid of the dark. So she sat up, smiled, and said, "I'm fine."

Everyone bowed their heads for silent prayer.

When the prayer was over, Sara reached for
the bowl of sugar and sprinkled some on her
eggs. She forked a piece of egg into her mouth
and spit it back out. "How come this *oi* [egg]
is so sweet?"

Solomon nudged Sara's arm. "You put *siesses* [sugar] on your egg."

Sara yawned. "I'm tired and didn't know what I was doing."

"Since you didn't get enough sleep," said Mom, "you'd better go to bed early tonight."

Sara frowned. She didn't want to go to bed early. She didn't want to go to bed at all!

That evening, Mom entered Sara's room and said, "It's time for bed."

Sara pointed to the puzzle she was working on. "I can't go to bed yet. This isn't done."

"You can finish it tomorrow," Mom said. "Put on your nightgown, wash your face, and brush your teeth. I'll be back soon to tuck you in bed."

Sara undressed and slipped her nightgown over her head. Then she knelt on the floor and peered under the bed.

"What are you looking for?" Mom asked when she stepped into the room.

"I can't find my doll," Sara said.

Mom pointed across the room. "She's there on the chair." She handed the doll to Sara. "Now hop into bed."

"I can't go to bed yet," Sara said with a shake of her head. "I didn't brush my teeth or wash my face."

Mom sighed. "You'd better run downstairs to the bathroom and do it now."

"Okay." Sara scampered out of the room.

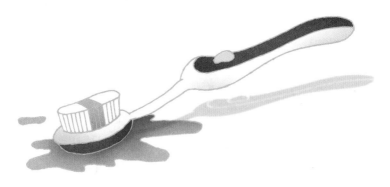

When Sara got to the bathroom she discovered the door was shut. *Bang! Bang! Bang!* She knocked on the door.

"Come back later," Paul called from the other side. "I'm busy brushing my teeth!"

Sara took a seat on the floor in the hall. She leaned against the wall and closed her eyes. Maybe Paul would stay in the bathroom all night. Then she could sleep out here and wouldn't have to go to bed in a dark, scary room.

A short time later, the bathroom door opened and Paul stepped out. "You can go in now, Sara."

Before Sara got to her feet, Mervin rushed into the bathroom and shut the door. Sara took a seat on the floor again. Maybe she would never have to go to bed.

The door finally opened, and Mervin
stepped out. "The bathroom's all yours," he said
with a grin.

Sarah looked around to see if anyone else
needed the bathroom, but there was no one
in sight. She waited a few more minutes, then
finally went inside.

Sara had just started brushing her teeth when—*Bang! Bang! Bang!*—someone knocked on the door. "Hurry up in there!" Solomon hollered, continuing to bang on the door.

"I'll be out in a minute!" Sara shouted.

Sometime later, Sara stepped out of the
bathroom, and Solomon rushed in.

"It's about time," he muttered.

Sara opened her mouth really wide. "I was
brushing my teeth. See how white they are?"

Solomon leaned close to Sara and squinted.
"You didn't clean them with *seef* [soap], I hope."

Sara shook her head. "Of course not."

Sara plodded up the stairs and into her room. She'd just climbed into bed when Mom entered and said, "Are you ready for bed?"

Sara nodded. "Can I leave the oil lantern lit tonight?"

"No, that would be dangerous." Mom snuffed out the light and kissed Sara's cheek. "Goodnight, sleepy head."

Sara closed her eyes and tried to sleep.
Whoosh! Whoosh!—the wind howled outside
her window. Sara's eyes snapped open. She
shivered as shadows danced on the wall. She
reached for the flashlight she kept by her bed.
Click! She shined the light around the room.
There, that was a little better.

Sara closed her eyes and was nearly asleep, when—*screetch. . .screetch*—something scraped against her window. Sara opened her eyes and gasped. The room was dark. The batteries in the flashlight must be dead!

Sara slipped out of bed. She needed to speak to Solomon. He was smart. Surely he would know what she should do.

Tap! Tap! Tap! Sara tapped on Solomon's door.

"Come in," said a sleepy voice.

Sara stepped into his room. Solomon clicked on his flashlight and shined the light on her.

"What do you want? Why aren't you in bed?"

Sara shivered. "The wind's blowing outside, and I'm afraid of the dark."

Solomon grabbed a pencil and a piece of
paper, then he wrote something down. "Here's
a verse from the Bible you can take with you to
bed." He handed her the paper. "It says: 'When
you lie down you will not be afraid; when you
lie down, your sleep will be sweet.'"

"Don't be afraid," said Solomon. "Jesus watches over you every night." He gave Sara his flashlight. "Take this so you can find your way in the dark."

"*Danki* [Thanks]," said Sara. She hurried to her room and climbed into bed. She placed the verse on her pillow.

"Good night, Jesus," Sara whispered, and she fell into a deep, sweet sleep.

A Friend in Need

*A generous man will himself be blessed,
for he shares his food with the poor.*

PROVERBS 22:9

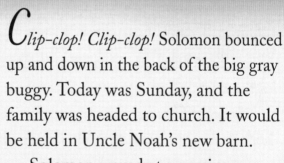

Clip-clop! Clip-clop! Solomon bounced up and down in the back of the big gray buggy. Today was Sunday, and the family was headed to church. It would be held in Uncle Noah's new barn.

Solomon waved at a passing car. *Beep! Beep!* The driver of the car honked his horn and waved back.

88

Dad pulled the horse and buggy into Uncle Noah's yard. "Remember, *kinner* [children]," he said, "be good and listen to everything in church."

"We will," the children all said. Solomon spotted his friends Willie and John under a tree and ran to greet them. "*Wie geht's* [How are you]?" he asked.

"I'm fine," said John. "Never better!"

Uncle Noah stepped up to them and smiled. "We're going inside for church now, boys. I hope you'll learn a lot today."

Solomon nodded. "I'll be listening."

Solomon and his friends found seats on a bench in the barn.

Solomon sang when it was time to sing. He prayed when it was time to pray.

"A generous man will himself be blessed,"
Uncle Noah said when he began his sermon.

Solomon's mind began to wander. Generous
meant giving and helpful. Blessed meant
favored with good things.

Hmm, thought Solomon, *if I'm generous, I'll
be blessed.*

When church was over, everyone ate lunch. After lunch, the men and women visited while the children played games.

"Let's go around back and swing," Willie suggested.

"That sounds like fun," Solomon said with a nod.

Solomon and his friends hurried to the swing.

"This is fun!" Solomon shouted when he took a turn. "I could swing like this the rest of the day!"

"You'd better not," said John. "I'd like a turn."

Solomon hopped off the swing. "Here you go, John!"

"Let's have a contest," Willie suggested.
"We'll see who can throw his hat the highest."

He removed his hat and tossed it in the
air—*whoosh!* When it came down, it landed in
a tree!

"Oh, fizzle," said Solomon. "Now what will
I do?"

Solomon stared up at Willie's hat.
If I get that hat, I'll be doing something good.

Solomon scampered up the tree. When he reached Willie's hat, he plunked it on his head and scampered back down. "Here you go!" Solomon grinned and handed the hat to Willie.

"*Danki* [Thanks]," said Willie.

John slowly shook his head. "You shouldn't have done that, Solomon. Climbing the tree was dangerous."

"I was being generous, like Uncle Noah said in his sermon. 'A generous man will himself be blessed.'" Solomon smiled. "Since I rescued your hat, I know I'll be blessed."

"I guess rescuing Willie's hat was a good thing," said John, "but there was more to that verse Uncle Noah read."

Solomon tipped his head. "There was?"

John nodded. "The verse said: 'A generous man will himself be blessed, for he shares his food with the poor.'"

"Oh," said Solomon with a frown. "I should have listened better. I need to find someone who's poor and do something generous."

Clip-clop. Clip-clop. Solomon glanced at the barn. "I see my *daed* [dad] is ready to go. I'll see you again soon!"

When Solomon's family arrived home, Solomon changed his clothes, took an apple from the refrigerator, and headed for the barn. He found their old horse Judy sleeping in her stall.

"Wake up!" he said, holding the apple under the horse's nose.

Judy opened one eye and gave a loud snort. *Chomp! Chomp!* She ate the juicy apple right to the core.

"What are you doing?" asked Paul, when he entered the stall.

Solomon grinned. "I'm doing what the Bible says. I'm feeding the poor."

Paul shook his head. "Judy's not poor."

Solomon reached under his hat and scratched his ear. "Then why does Mom call the horse, 'poor old Judy'?"

Paul leaned his head back and laughed. "Because Judy's getting old and feeble," he said.

Solomon felt the heat of a blush.

So much for sharing his food with the poor!

On the way to school one day, Solomon
noticed his English neighbor, David, waiting for
the bus.

Sara nudged Solomon. "Have you noticed
that David hasn't carried a lunch pail all week?"

Solomon frowned and shook his head. "I'll
be right back."

"Where are you going?" asked Sara.

"To speak with David. Go on ahead."

Solomon crossed the road and stepped up to David. "Hi, how are you?"

"Not so good," David mumbled.

"How come?" asked Solomon.

David looked at Solomon with sorrowful brown eyes. "My dad's been out of work for almost a month. Since we don't have much money, I don't have any lunch."

Solomon thought about the Bible verse Uncle Noah had read in church. Solomon smiled and handed David his lunch pail. "You can have my lunch."

David's eyes opened wide. "You're giving me your lunch?"

Solomon nodded. "I had a big breakfast, so I won't miss not eating lunch."

David's chin trembled, and tears slid down his cheeks. "Thank you, Solomon. You're a good friend."

Solomon smiled, already feeling blessed. "You're welcome."

That evening during supper, Solomon told everyone about David's dad being out of work.

"David didn't have a lunch to take to school," he said.

"That's a shame," said Mom. "We need to help David's family."

Sara nodded. "Solomon already did. He gave David his lunch pail."

Dad patted Solomon's back. "That was thoughtful of you, son."

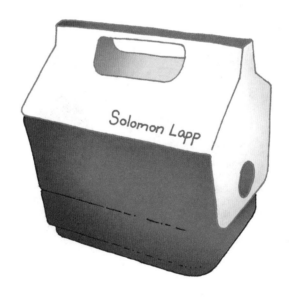

Solomon's face grew warm. "I just did what the Bible says."

"Maybe we should take David's family a basket of food," Mom suggested.

Dad nodded. "That's a good idea. I'll speak to some others and see about getting David's family help with food, money, and anything else they need."

Solomon leaned back in his chair and smiled. Helping David made him feel warm inside, and it made him want to be the kind of person who would always look for ways to be generous to others.

Father Knows Best

A wise son heeds his father's instruction.   PROVERBS 13:1

I'd like you to feed the chickens,"
Mom told Solomon after breakfast
one morning.

"Be sure to feed them inside the coop,"
Dad said.

Solomon's eyebrows pulled
together. "Can't I feed them outside?"

109

Dad shook his head. "I built new nesting boxes yesterday, and I want the chickens to lay their eggs in the boxes." He patted the top of Solomon's head. "Remember Solomon. . .a wise son listens to his father's instruction."

When Solomon entered the chicken coop, none of the chickens were there. He stepped outside and looked around the yard. Some chickens were in the pasture. Some were near the barn. Some sat on the fence.

"If I take the time to get the chickens back in the coop, there'll be no time to play," said Solomon.

Solomon scratched his head and thought about the situation. "If I feed the chickens outside, I can put them in the coop when they're done eating."

He grabbed the bucket of chicken feed and tossed it on the ground. *Bawk! Bawk! Bawk!* The chickens gathered around the food and gobbled it right up.

When the food was all gone, Solomon opened the door of the coop. "Here chick, chick, chick!" he called. The chickens all scattered. Some went to the pasture. Some went to the barn. Some flew to the fence.

Solomon shrugged. "I guess they'll go to the coop whenever they're ready."

"Would you please go out to the chicken coop and check for eggs?" Mom asked Solomon the following day.

Solomon took the egg basket and headed out the door. When he entered the coop, he looked in every nesting box, but there were no eggs. He scratched his head and thought, *Now that's sure strange.*

Solomon rushed back to the house. "There were no eggs this morning," he told Mom.

Her forehead wrinkled. "No eggs at all?"

Solomon shook his head. "All the boxes were empty."

Just then, Mervin stepped into the room. "Look what I found under a bush in the yard!" He held a dirty egg in each hand.

Dad looked at Solomon. "Where did you feed the chickens yesterday?"

A trickle of sweat rolled down Solomon's brow. "I—uh—fed them outside."

Dad frowned and tapped his foot. "Next time please do as I say."

That afternoon Solomon went to the barn to get his fishing pole.

"There's something I need you to do," Dad said.

Solomon held up the pole. "I was planning to do some fishing."

"You can do that when you're finished feeding the goats," Dad said. "And be sure to latch the gate when you're done."

Solomon leaned his fishing pole against the wall and hurried to the goat pen. He quickly fed the goats then grabbed his pole.

"I'm heading to the creek. Do you want to come along?" he asked Sara and Mervin, who were jumping on the trampoline.

"No thanks," Sara said. "We're having too much fun!"

As soon as Solomon reached the creek, he took a seat on the grass and threw his line in the water.

He'd only been there a few minutes when he heard Mom holler, "Get away from my garden you troublesome *gees* [goats]!"

Solomon set his fishing pole aside and scrambled to his feet.

When Solomon got to the yard, he saw Mom chasing one of their goats.

"*Absatz* [Stop]!" she shouted. "You'd better not eat any more of my garden!"

Solomon ran after the goat and chased him back to his pen.

"Didn't you latch the gate after you fed the goats?" Mom asked.

Solomon's face grew hot. "Dad told me to latch it, but I was in a hurry to get to the creek, and I must have forgotten."

Mom pointed to the garden, where rows of peas had once been. "This is what happens when you don't listen to your father. Now you'll have to plant more peas!"

Solomon spent the next hour on his knees, planting several rows of peas. It was hard to work in the hot sun while Sara and Mervin ran around the yard blowing bubbles and playing tag.

Solomon had just finished planting when his brother Clarence showed up. "Dad wants you to go out to the pasture and bring in the horses," Clarence said.

"Why can't you do it?" Solomon asked.

"Because I'm heading to the house to get a jug of water, and then I need to get back to the fields."

Clarence started to walk away but turned back around. "Dad said to remind you not to go near the pasture where the bull is grazing."

Solomon hurried off. If he got the horses brought in right away, he might have time to do some fishing before supper.

As Solomon neared the pasture, he noticed Grumpy the bull lying by the fence on the far side of the pasture. Since Grumpy was obviously asleep, Solomon thought it would be okay for him to take a shortcut to the horses' pasture.

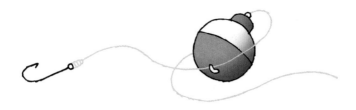

Solomon climbed the fence and was halfway across the pasture, when the bull jumped up and charged after him. Solomon ran as fast as he could.

Thump! Thump! Thump! The bull came so close Solomon could feel his hot breath.

Solomon dashed over to the closest tree and climbed to the highest branch.

"Help! Help!" he hollered.

The bull snorted and pawed at the ground.

Solomon hung onto the tree branch and prayed for help to come. His arms ached, and his voice grew hoarse from yelling. He was sure he'd be stuck in the tree forever.

Just then Solomon spotted Dad and Clarence, waving their arms and running across the pasture.

The bull turned and ran to the other side.
On shaky legs, Solomon climbed down from
the tree. "I–I'm sorry for not listening," he said
with tears running down his cheeks. "I shouldn't
have gone anywhere near that bull!"

Dad bent down and gave Solomon a hug. "That's right, you should have listened, because a wise son heeds his father's instruction."

Solomon nodded and squeezed Dad's neck. "From now on, I promise to do whatever I'm told."

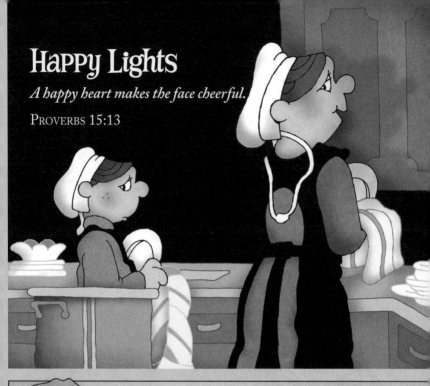

Happy Lights

A happy heart makes the face cheerful.

PROVERBS 15:13

"Why do you look so sad?" Mom asked Sara as they washed and dried the supper dishes.

"It's hot, and I'm bored," Sara complained.

Mom touched Sara's cheek. "The Bible tells us that a happy heart makes our face cheerful. Why don't you think of something fun to do?"

130

"I can't think of anything fun," Sara said as she dried the last dish and put it away.

Mom smiled. "I have an idea. Why don't you go outside and catch some happy lights?"

Sara tipped her head. "What are happy lights?"

Mom pointed out the window. "When my sisters and I were girls, and one of us was in a bad mood, our *mamm* [mom] sent us outside to catch fireflies." Mom chuckled. "We called the fireflies 'happy lights' because we had so much fun trying to catch them."

Mom handed Sara an empty canning jar. "If you catch some happy lights, you can put them in this."

Sara took the jar and went out the door. She found Solomon and Mervin sitting on the front porch.

"Would you like to catch some happy lights with me?" she asked her brothers.

"What are happy lights?" Mervin wanted to know.

"I'm talking about fireflies," Sara replied.

"Some people call them lightning bugs," Solomon said, "but I've never heard them called happy lights before."

"We'll find out why when we catch them," Sara said.

Mervin jumped up and down. "*Jah* [Yes]! This should be fun!"

Solomon grabbed Mervin's hand, and they all ran into the yard.

"Keep your eyes on the grass," Solomon said.

Mervin crouched down and stared at the lawn. "I don't see a thing," he said with a shake of his head.

"Be patient and wait. I'm sure we'll see some fireflies soon," Sara said.

A few minutes later, she pointed to the shimmering fireflies rising from the grass. "Here they come now, so let's see how quickly we can fill up the jar!"

Solomon darted to the left. Sara scurried to the right. Mervin crawled across the middle of the lawn.

"Oh no!" Solomon hollered as he leaped into the air. "I missed that one!"

Sara giggled when a firefly landed on her hand. She picked it up and dropped it into the jar.

Mervin crawled over to Sara and grabbed the glass jar. "I've got two!" he shouted.

"Catching happy lights sure is fun!" Sara nodded and added five more fireflies. Soon, the whole jar was lit up with glowing bugs.

Sara, Solomon, and Mervin sat on the porch and watched the fireflies awhile; then they opened the jar and let them go free.

When Mom called them in for bed, they raced into the house wearing happy faces.

Sara scurried up the stairs to her room and looked out her bedroom window at the starry sky. *More happy lights to look at,* she thought. It felt good to smile and think happy thoughts. It was much better than being gloomy.

A few days later, Sara's friend Ellen Miller came over to spend the night. Ellen entered Sara's bedroom with a sour look on her face. Sara figured her friend must be in a grumpy mood.

"What's wrong?" Sara asked. "Aren't you happy to be here spending the night?"

Ellen's lower lip stuck out. "If my mamm hadn't just had a *boppli* [baby], we would have gone camping today."

"I'm sure you'll go camping some other time," Sara said. She took a seat on the bed beside Ellen. "Having a new boppli in the family is exciting. You should be happy, not sad."

Ellen's shoulders slumped. "What if my mamm and *daed* [dad] love the boppli more than me?"

Sara shook her head. "I'm sure they won't. My mamm and daed love all their *kinner* [children] the same."

Ellen crossed her arms and stared at the floor. Sara had never seen her friend so gloomy before. She wished there was something she could do to put Ellen in a better mood.

"Why don't we do something fun?" she suggested.

Ellen shook her head. "It's too hot in here to do anything fun."

Sara tapped her finger against her chin as she thought and thought. Suddenly she remembered the verse of scripture Mom had mentioned not long ago: "A happy heart makes the face cheerful."

Sara grabbed Ellen's hand and gave it a tug. "Let's go outside and catch some happy lights!"

Ellen wrinkled her forehead. "What are happy lights?"

Sara smiled. "If you come with me, you'll find out."

As Sara and Ellen passed through the kitchen, Sara grabbed an empty canning jar and led Ellen out the door. They found Solomon and Mervin on the porch.

"Would you two like to help us catch some happy lights?" Sara asked.

"Jah, of course!" both boys said.

Solomon darted to the left. Sara scurried to the right. Mervin crawled across the middle of the lawn. Ellen watched, still wearing a frown.

"Come back here!" Solomon hollered as he leaped into the air. "I always miss the first one!"

Sara giggled as she grabbed a firefly and dropped it into the glass jar.

"Come help us look for fireflies," Solomon
called to Sara's friend.

Ellen bent down, picked up two fireflies, and
put them in the jar. "This is fun!" she said with
a chuckle. "I'm having a good time catching
happy lights!"

Sara nodded and gave Ellen a hug. "It's good to have a happy heart and wear a cheerful face." She looked over at Solomon and smiled. "It's good for us to help others look on the bright side of things!"

Good-bye, Judy

An anxious heart weighs a man down.

PROVERBS 12:25

*Y*ou're a good horse, Judy," Solomon said as he stood by the fence stroking their buggy horse's nose.

"What are you doing?" Clarence asked when he joined Solomon on the fence.

"I'm petting Judy," Solomon said. "I was worried about her. She looked lonely."

Clarence thumped Solomon's shoulder. "You shouldn't worry. The Bible says 'an anxious heart weighs a man down.'" He stepped off the fence. "I'd better go. I don't have time to pet this old, slow horse."

Solomon patted Judy's head. "You're not old, and you're not slow." Judy whinnied and licked Solomon's hand with her big, rough tongue.

Later that day, Solomon climbed on his scooter and went to get the mail. He found an envelope that wasn't sealed. Suddenly, a gust of wind sent the letter flying. Solomon jumped off the scooter and raced up the driveway. *Woosh!*—the letter sailed out of the envelope.

"Uh-oh!" Solomon said.

Solomon grabbed the letter just before it landed in the horses' watering trough. "Whew, that was close."

As he carried the letter to the house, he noticed some of the words:

Good. . .buy. . .sell. . .Judy.

Solomon's heart pounded. Was Dad planning to sell Judy? Did he think she was old and slow, like Clarence said?

Solomon ran to the house. He dropped the letter on the table and raced outside.

Solomon ran to the trampoline where Sara and Mervin were jumping.

"I need to talk to you, Sara."

Sara climbed off the trampoline. Solomon led her to the pasture, where Judy slept in a clump of grass.

"Dad's going to sell Judy!"

Sara's mouth dropped open. "How do you know?"

"When I went to get the mail, a letter blew away; and when I got it, I read some of the words. They said: Good, buy, sell, Judy." Solomon slowly shook his head. "Dad must have Judy up for sale. Whoever wrote the letter wants to buy her."

Sara's eyes filled with tears. "We have to do something. We can't let Dad sell Judy."

Solomon paced from the barn to the watering trough. "I can't think of anything now, but I'll keep thinking."

The Lapps
77 North Star Rd.
Lancaster, PA 17572

When Solomon went to bed that night, he lay awake, worrying and thinking about Judy.

When he got up the next morning, he was so tired he could barely stand. During breakfast, Solomon almost fell asleep while eating his cereal.

"Did you come up with a way to save Judy?"
Sara asked as they walked to school.

Solomon scratched his head. "Not yet, but
by the time we get home from school, I should
have a plan."

"You don't look well," said John when Solomon got to school. "Are you feeling *grank* [sick]?"

"I'm not sick," Solomon said. "I'm worried about our buggy horse."

"What's wrong with Judy?" asked John.

"She's about to be sold," said Solomon. "I have to come up with a way to keep her."

"Why don't you hide Judy someplace where no one can find her?" John suggested.

Solomon jumped up and down and whirled around. "That's a *wunderbaar* [wonderful] idea! I'll hide Judy in the woods!"

When Solomon got home, he dashed into the barn. Judy wasn't there! Solomon rushed out the door and climbed the fence. Dad's work horses were in the pasture, but there was no sign of Judy.

"Oh no, Dad's already sold her!" he moaned. "What if Judy gets homesick and doesn't eat or drink? I'm so worried about Judy!"

As Solomon trudged toward the house, he spotted Sara.

"I just came from the barn, but Judy wasn't there," Sara said.

Solomon nodded. "Judy's not in the pasture, either. I think Dad sold her while we were at school."

Sara's mouth turned down at the corners. "Good-bye, Judy. I'll miss you."

With heads down and shoulders slumped, Solomon and Sara shuffled into the house.

"How was school?" Mom asked.

Solomon shrugged. Sara sniffed and wiped her nose.

"What's wrong? You look like you've lost your best friend," Mom said.

"We have," Solomon mumbled as he sank into a chair with a groan.

"Which friend did you lose?" Mom asked.

"Judy," Solomon replied.

"I didn't know there was anyone at school named Judy," said Mom.

Solomon shook his head. "I'm talking about our buggy horse. Dad sold her while we were at school."

Mom's eyebrows shot up. "Your *daed* [dad] sold Judy?" She raced for the back door, but before she could open it, Dad and Clarence stepped in.

"We're back!" Dad said with a smile.

Mom gave Dad's shirtsleeve a tug. "How could you do such a thing?"

Dad's forehead wrinkled. "What?"

166

"How could you sell Judy?" Mom asked.

Dad gave his beard a couple of pulls. "I don't know what you're talking about. Clarence and I just put Judy in the barn."

"She wasn't there a few minutes ago," said Sara.

"She wasn't in the pasture, either," said Solomon.

Dad nodded. "That's because she was at Harvey Yoder's getting new shoes."

Solomon blew out his breath, lifting the hair off his forehead. "I saw some words on the letter you got yesterday. I was sure you were going to sell Judy."

"What words?" Dad asked.

"Good, buy, sell, Judy," Solomon said.

Dad laughed so hard his beard jiggled up and down. "The letter was from my brother Sam. He said our cousin Judy got a good buy on a new house, and she's going to sell her old one."

"I guess I was worried for nothing," Solomon said.

Clarence thumped Solomon's back. "An anxious heart weighs a man down. Next time you're worried you should pray, and then tell Mom and Dad."

"*Jah* [Yes], I will."

Solomon motioned to the fruit bowl on the table. "May I have an apple?"

Mom nodded.

Solomon grabbed an apple and raced for the door.

When Solomon got to the barn, he opened
the door to Judy's stall and held out his hand.

Judy opened her big mouth and chomped
the apple.

When Solomon headed out of the barn, he
looked over his shoulder. "Good-bye, Judy," he
whispered. "I'll see you tomorrow."

A True Friend

A friend loves at all times.

Proverbs 17:17

$\mathcal{S}$olomon whistled as he headed
for the barn to do his chores.

Meow! A yellow cat darted out of
the barn. Its hair stood up. Its ears
went straight back. Solomon knew
something must have happened to
frighten the poor cat.

172

Solomon hurried into the barn. He spotted Mervin laughing and chasing a fluffy white cat around some bales of straw.

Just as Mervin reached out to pull the cat's tail, Solomon shouted, *"Absatz* [Stop]!"

The cat zipped between Mervin's legs and darted out of the barn.

Solomon shook his finger at Mervin. "Didn't you hear the Bible verse Dad read to us last night?"

Mervin shrugged his shoulders. "I forgot. What'd it say?"

"A friend loves at all times." Solomon motioned to the chickens. "Animals are like friends and should be treated kindly."

Mervin nodded and scurried out of the barn.

When Solomon left the barn a short time later, he noticed Mervin running around the yard.

Bawk! Bawk! Chickens ran everywhere, squawking and flapping their wings. Some ran to the left. Some ran to the right. Mervin chased after them, waving his hands.

"Absatz!" shouted Solomon. "Stop chasing those chickens!"

Mervin skidded to a halt. "I was just having a little fun."

Solomon frowned and shook his head. "Remember, we must be kind to our animal friends."

"I forgot," said Mervin. He raced across the yard and climbed onto the trampoline.

Solomon gave the chickens food and water, then he headed for the house.

Later that day, Solomon went to the barn to milk the cows. He'd just pulled out the milking pail when several pieces of straw landed on the cow's head.

The cow twitched its ear and let out a loud, *Moo-oo!*

Solomon looked up. Mervin was in the hayloft holding some straw.

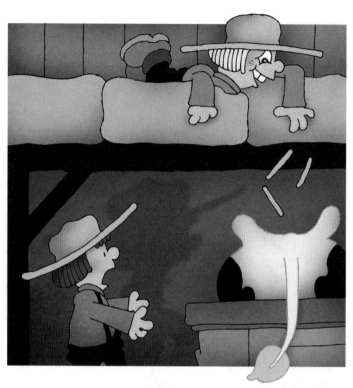

"What are you doing?" Solomon called to his brother. "Why are you dropping straw on the cow?"

Mervin snickered. "It's fun to watch the cow's ears twitch."

"A friend loves at all times," Solomon said.

Mervin nodded and climbed down the ladder.

That night after supper, Mom asked Mervin to take their dog, Butch, a bone.

Mervin grabbed the bone and ran out the door.

"Solomon, would you go outside and make sure Mervin does what I asked?" Mom frowned. "Sometimes he gets distracted and forgets to do as he's told."

Solomon headed out the door. He found Mervin in the yard, holding the bone above the dog's head.

Woof! Woof! Butch leaped into the air, but the bone was out of his reach.

"Absatz!" Solomon shouted. "Why are you teasing the dog?"

Mervin's face turned red. "I was only teasing a bit."

Solomon took the bone and gave it to the dog. Butch scampered off to his doghouse.

Solomon turned to Mervin and said, "A friend loves at all times."

Mervin hung his head. "*Jah* [Yes], I know. I'll try to do better from now on."

For the next several days, Solomon kept an eye on his little brother. Once, he spotted Mervin feeding the cats. Another time, he saw Mervin giving water to the cows. Solomon noticed Mervin on the back porch, petting Butch. Solomon smiled and went into the house.

The next day, Solomon had just started painting the fence, when his friend Willie rode into the yard in his pony cart.

"*Wie geht's* [How are you]?" Willie asked.
"I'm fine. Just busy," Solomon said.

Willie leaned on the fence.

"Don't get too close," Solomon said. He pointed to the paint bucket by his feet. "You might get paint on your clothes."

Willie stepped back. "I came to ask you a question."

"Uh-huh," Solomon mumbled, as he brushed more paint on the fence.

Willie smiled and stepped forward.

"I was wondering if—"

"I told you not to get too close!" Solomon frowned. "Why didn't you listen?"

Willie shrugged. "I did listen, but I wanted to be sure you heard what I said."

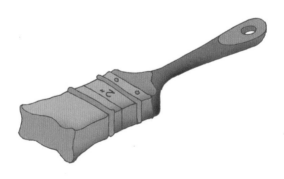

"I heard you just fine." Solomon waved his paint brush in the air. "Can't you see that I'm busy?"

"I guess if you're too busy to talk to your friend, I'll head for home."

Willie climbed into his pony cart and rode away. Solomon continued to paint the fence.

The next day Solomon helped his brother
Paul clean the horses' stalls. Dad had told
Solomon if he hurried and got the job done he
could play.

Swish! Swish! Solomon swept the broom
across the cement floor.

"Wie geht's?" said Willie as he stepped into the barn.

"I'm fine," said Solomon, "but I'm very busy."

"There's something I need to ask you," Willie said. He leaned on the door to the horses' stall.

Solomon shook his head. "Not now. I've got too much to do."

Willie turned and shuffled out of the barn.

After church on Sunday, Sara stepped up to Solomon and said, "Did you notice how sad Willie looks today?"

Solomon shook his head. "I really hadn't noticed."

"I asked him what was wrong," Sara said. "He said he's sad because you're not his friend anymore."

"That's *lecherich* [ridiculous]," said Solomon. "Willie's still my friend."

Sara pointed across the yard, where Willie sat under a tree. "Maybe you should tell him that."

Solomon hurried across the yard.

"Wie geht's?" he asked when he flopped on the ground beside Willie.

Willie shrugged. "I'd be better if I knew we were still friends."

"Why would you think we weren't friends?" asked Solomon.

Willie frowned. "The last few times I've come to visit, you were too busy to talk to me."

Solomon hung his head in shame. "I'm sorry, Willie. I've been telling Mervin to treat his animal friends better, while I've been ignoring you. Will you forgive me?"

Willie nodded.

The next day, Willie came to see Solomon again.

"This is for you," he said, handing Solomon a floppy-eared puppy.

"*Danki* [Thanks]." Solomon hugged the puppy, then he gave Willie a hug, too. "A true friend loves at all times, and I'm going to be the best friend I can be!"

Payback

Do not say, "I'll do to him as he had done to me; I'll pay that man back for what he did."

PROVERBS 24:29

Uncle Noah preached a good sermon today," Dad said as the Lapps traveled home from church in their buggy. He glanced over his shoulder and smiled. "Didn't you think so, Solomon?"

Solomon nodded. "Uncle Noah always preaches good sermons. I hope I grow up to be just like him."

That night, as Solomon got ready for bed, a knock sounded on the door. "Come in," Solomon called.

The door opened, and Sara rushed into the room holding her doll. "Little sister Katie tore my doll's dress," she cried. "I'm going to pay her back for what she did."

Solomon shook his head. "Remember what Uncle Noah said in church today?"

"*Nee* [No]," said Sara. "What did he say?"

Solomon pointed to the Bible on the table beside his bed. "God's Word says we shouldn't pay others back for what they've done. You need to forgive Katie for tearing your doll's dress."

Solomon handed Sara a handkerchief, and she blew her nose with a loud *honk!*

"I'm sure Mom will make a new dress for your doll," Solomon said.

Sara smiled and skipped out of the room. "I won't pay Katie back. I'll forgive her instead!"

Solomon hopped into bed, pulled the covers up to his chin, and drifted off to sleep.

The next morning, Solomon
went to the goat pen to feed his
goat, Mary. "That's strange—
Mary's not here," he said as he
scratched his head.

Solomon looked everywhere for Mary.
He looked on the porch. He looked in the barn.
He looked by the clothesline on the side of the
house. There was no sign of Mary anywhere!

Solomon ran out to the pasture and called for his goat. No Mary there, either. "Maybe she got into Mom's garden. *Ach* [Oh], I hope she didn't eat the tomatoes or lettuce. That would be *baremlich* [terrible]!"

Solomon dashed over to the garden. No Mary there—just a fat little frog poking its head out from under a cabbage plant.

"Good grief," said Solomon. "Where in the world could my goat be?"

Solomon sprinted down the driveway. He looked to the left. He looked to the right. No Mary in sight.

Solomon cupped his hands around his mouth. "Mary! Where are you?"

Ma-a-a! Ma-a-a!

Solomon tipped his head and listened.

Ma-a-a! Ma-a-a!

He was sure it was Mary calling to him.

Solomon ran down the path leading to their neighbor's house. "Where are you, Mary?" he called.

Ma-a-a! Ma-a-a! The farther Solomon went, the closer Mary sounded.

He spotted Mrs. Stoltzfus running around the yard, waving her hands. "Let go of my quilt, you naughty goat!" she shouted.

Solomon raced into the yard. There was Mary, dragging a colorful quilt through the grass.

"Drop that quilt!" Solomon hollered as he chased after the goat. Mary leaped into the air, dropped the quilt on the ground, and let out a loud, *Ma-a-a!*

Solomon crept forward. His fingers almost touched Mary's collar, when she scurried away.

Whoosh!— she grabbed one of Mrs. Stoltzfus's towels off the clothesline—*rip!* Around and around the yard Mary went, swishing her tail and dragging the towel through the dirt.

"Drop that towel, you naughty goat!" Mrs. Stoltzfus hollered.

Mary skidded to a stop, dropped the towel in the dirt, and leaped onto the porch.

Solomon raced after her. He was almost to the porch, when—*crash!*—Mary knocked over a pot of pansies.

Mrs. Stoltzfus gasped and squinted her eyes at Solomon. "Is that your goat?"

Solomon nodded. "I don't know how she got out of her pen."

Mrs. Stoltzfus pointed at Mary and frowned. "Thanks to your naughty goat, my quilt's dirty, my towel's ripped, and my flower pot's broken."

"I'm sorry," Solomon said. "I'll take Mary home, then I'll come back and work for you to make up for the damage my goat did to your things."

Mrs. Stoltzfus nodded. "I appreciate that."

Solomon grabbed Mary's collar and led her toward home. He'd only gone a short ways when he heard snickering in the bushes.

"Hee-hee! Ha-ha! I got you good," Cousin Abe said as he popped his head out of a bush.

Solomon tapped his foot and glared at Abe. "Did you take my goat and put her in Mrs. Stoltzfus's yard?"

Abe nodded and held his sides.

"Hee-hee! Ha-ha! I played a good trick on you!"

Solomon frowned.

"Thanks to you, my goat ruined some of Mrs. Stoltzfus's things. Now I'll have to work for her the rest of the morning to clean it all up."

"I'm sorry," said Abe. "I was only playing a joke. I didn't know the goat would do anything bad."

Abe ran off before Solomon could say another word.

"I'll pay you back for what you did," Solomon mumbled as he pulled Mary along.

All the way home, Solomon thought about Abe's mean trick. "It's not right. It's not fair," he fretted and fumed.

Solomon kicked a stone with his shoe. "I should do something mean to pay Abe back for what he did!"

Solomon was about to put Mary back in her pen, when Mervin rushed up and pulled her tail.

"Why'd you do that?" Solomon asked.

Mervin frowned. "That naughty goat butted my leg last night, so I'm paying her back."

Suddenly, Solomon remembered the verse Uncle Noah had read during church on Sunday. "It's wrong to pay someone back for what they've done," he said.

Mervin tipped his head. "Even a goat?"

Solomon nodded. "Even a goat—or your sneaky cousin who likes to play tricks."

Solomon knew if he paid Abe back for letting Mary loose it would be wrong. If he wanted to grow up to be like Uncle Noah, he would have to forgive Cousin Abe and forget the whole thing ever happened.

"Let's put Mary in her pen and go get something to eat," Solomon said. "After breakfast we have some work to do for Mrs. Stoltzfus." Solomon took Mervin's hand. "And no more pulling Mary's tail!"

Stretching the Truth

A truthful witness does not deceive, but a false witness pours out lies.

PROVERBS 14:5

"Solomon, come quick! There's a creepy-looking spider in my room, and it's big as a horse!"

Sara tugged on Solomon's sleeve. "Will you get it for me?"

Solomon shook his head. "Spiders don't get as big as a horse. You shouldn't stretch the truth. It's almost the same as telling a lie."

214

Sara's lower lip jutted out. "Does that mean you won't get the spider for me?"

"Why don't you get it yourself?" Solomon asked.

Sara shivered and shook her head. "I could never do that. I'm afraid of spiders."

"That's *lecherich* [ridiculous]," Solomon said. "You're bigger than the spider."

Sara wrinkled her nose. "I won't go near that creepy creature!"

"Oh, fine," Solomon said with a groan. "I'll get the spider!"

He followed Sara to her room. "Where is this big bug?"

"It's over there." Sara pointed to the window. "Before I came to get you, it was crawling along the ledge. If you don't get that spider, it's gonna eat everything in my room!"

Solomon nudged Sara. "You're stretching the truth."

"No, I'm not! There it is!" Sara hollered.

Solomon moved closer to the window. "That little bitty thing? It's no bigger than my thumb!"

The spider moved. Sara jumped.

Solomon opened the window. He picked up the spider, and set it outside on the limb of a tree.

Sara sighed with relief.

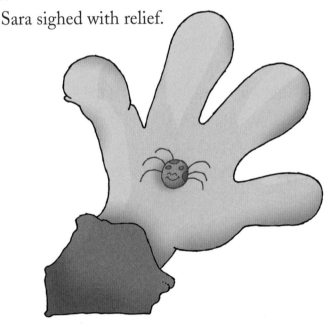

A few days later, Sara and Solomon were doing the supper dishes.

"Washing dishes isn't much fun," Solomon grumbled as he sloshed the dishrag along the edge of a plate. "I'd rather be outside playing with my puppy."

Sara nodded. "If we hurry and get the dishes done, we'll have time to play before we go to bed."

Solomon gave Sara a plate to dry. *Swish! Swish!* She swiped the dishcloth across the plate. *Whoosh!*—it slipped out of her hand and landed on the floor with a *crash!*

"Oh, no!" Sara moaned. "That was one of Mom's favorite dishes!" She dropped to her knees and picked up the pieces. Then she dumped them in the garbage can.

"I'm not gonna tell Mom about the plate," Sara said.

Solomon frowned. "If you don't tell her, it'll be the same as lying."

Tears streamed down Sara's face. "Please don't say anything."

Solomon scratched the side of his head. "If you give it some thought, you'll realize that telling the truth is the right thing to do."

On Saturday, Sara's friend Betty Miller came over to play. "Would you like to jump on the trampoline?" asked Sara.

Betty shook her head. "It's hard to keep my balance."

"Would you like to play with my doll?" asked Sara.

Betty shook her head. "I don't like playing with dolls that much."

"What would you like to do?" Sara asked.

Betty pointed to a bright green yo-yo on the shelf near the back door. "I'd like to play with that."

Sara nibbled on her lip as she thought. The yo-yo was Solomon's. She knew she should ask him if Betty could play with it, but Solomon wasn't home. He'd gone to his friend John's house to play.

"Can I play with the yo-yo?" Betty asked again.

Sara nodded. "All right, but be careful with it."

Zip! Zip! Betty made the yo-yo go up and down. "*Ach* [Oh], this sure is fun!"

Pop!—the string broke! The yo-yo flew into the flowerbed. Sara frowned.

After Betty went home, Sara raced into the barn. She hid the yo-yo in a mound of hay.

A short time later, Solomon came home.

He'd just begun feeding the horses, when he shouted, "Who broke my yo-yo string and hid it in the hay?"

"I have no idea," Sara said. "Maybe Grandpa will buy you a new one."

As Sara and Solomon walked to school on Monday morning, Sara noticed some pretty flowers growing along the path. "I think I'll pick a few flowers to give our teacher," she said.

"You'd better not, or we might be late," said Solomon.

Sara shook her head. "We have all morning to get to school."

Solomon grunted. "No, we don't, and you're stretching the truth! You should be careful what you say and do."

Sara picked one flower, and then another. "I don't see what's wrong with stretching the truth. It's not like I'm hurting anyone."

Solomon reached into his backpack and took out a rubber band. "If I stretch this until it snaps, it can hurt really bad. The same thing happens when a person lies or stretches the truth."

Sara shrugged and started walking again. She figured Solomon liked telling her what to do.

By the time Sara and Solomon got to school, the flowers had wilted. Sara gave them to Teacher Naomi anyway.

"*Danki* [Thanks]," Naomi said. She put them in a jar of water and placed them on her desk.

Sara smiled and hurried to her seat.

Rr Ss Tt Uu Vv Ww

Later that morning, when Sara was taking a math test, her pencil broke. She knew Naomi didn't like anyone to get out of their seat during a test, but she needed a pencil.

"*Psst...*" Sara tapped Betty on the shoulder. "Do you have a pencil I can borrow?" she asked.

Betty nodded. "I have an extra one in my desk." She opened the lid and removed a pencil. "Here you go."

"Ah-hem!" Teacher Naomi cleared her throat. "Betty Miller, you know better than to talk during a test."

Betty's face turned red. "I was just—"

Naomi clapped her hands. "No more talking, or I'll keep you after school!"

Tears sprang to Betty's eyes. "Sara was talking, too. She asked me for a pencil."

Naomi looked at Sara. "Is that true?"

Thump! Thump! Thump! Sara's heart pounded. She was afraid if she told the truth she would be punished. If she lied, Betty would be in trouble.

I've stretched the truth too many times, Sara thought. She looked at the teacher and said, "My pencil broke, and I asked if I could borrow one of Betty's."

Naomi tapped Sara's shoulder. "Next time you need something during a test, raise your hand and ask me, not Betty."

Sara nodded. "I will, Teacher."

After school, Sara said to Solomon, "When we get home I'm gonna tell Mom about the broken plate. Oh, and there's something I need to tell you as well. . . ."

"What do you need to tell me?" Solomon asked.

"I let Betty play with your yo-yo," Sara replied. "The string broke, and I hid it. Will you forgive me?"

Solomon nodded and gave her a hug. "Telling the truth is the right thing to do."

Even a Child

Even a child is known by his actions.

<small>Proverbs</small> 20:11

$\mathcal{S}$olomon whistled as he pulled his wagon toward town. Mom had asked him to pick up a few things at the grocery store.

Solomon reached into his pocket and jiggled the money. Mom had given him a few extra coins to buy something for himself.

235

Birds whistled and chirped from the trees along the road. *Ribbit! Ribbit!* A frog croaked as it hopped along the path.

Solomon smiled. It looked like he wasn't the only one in a good mood this morning.

As Solomon continued along, he saw his English neighbor, David, playing in his yard. Solomon waved and hollered, "Good morning, David. How are things with you and your family these days?"

David waved back.
"Things are good.
Dad has a new job.
Now we can buy
groceries and pay
our bills."

Solomon smiled. He was glad he and his
family had helped with food and money when
David's dad was out of work.

Clip-clop. Clip-clop. Solomon heard a horse and buggy coming down the road.

"Where are you headed?" asked Uncle Noah as his buggy came alongside of Solomon.

"I'm going to Bird-in-Hand to do some shopping for my *mamm* [mom]."

Uncle Noah smiled. "You're a good boy
for helping. The Bible says that even a child
is known by his actions. A wise boy like you
should set a good example for others."

Uncle Noah waved and headed down the
road. *Clip-clop. Clip-clop.*

When Solomon arrived at the grocery store, he discovered that some things on his list cost more than he'd expected. It took all the money in his pocket to pay for the items he bought.

"Now I won't be able to go to the bakery and buy a donut," he mumbled as he went out the door.

Solomon put the sacks of groceries into the wagon. When he looked up, he noticed an elderly woman coming out of the store carrying two paper sacks. When the door closed, it bumped her arm. One of the sacks tipped over, spilling all her groceries onto the ground.

Solomon rushed forward. "Here, let me help!" He dropped to his knees and quickly picked up the items; then he put them back in the sack.

"Would you like me to carry the groceries to your car?" he asked the woman.

"That would be nice," she said with a nod. When they got to her car, she reached into her purse and handed Solomon fifty cents. "This is for being so helpful and kind."

Solomon shook his head. "Oh no! You don't have to pay me."

The woman smiled and patted Solomon's arm. "I want you to keep the money."

"Thank you," said Solomon. "I think I'll visit the bakery now."

A short time later, Solomon headed down the road, pulling his wagon and chomping on a chocolate donut. When he arrived home, he helped Mom put away the groceries.

"*Danki* [Thanks]," she said. "I'm pleased that you're willing to help."

Solomon smiled. "Can I go outside now and play?"

Mom nodded and gave him a hug.

Solomon went straight to the barn. He found the puppy he'd named Peaches there, asleep in some straw.

"I feel good about the helpful things I've done today," he said as he stroked the puppy's ear. "I'm going to look for kind things to do every day."

"I can't wait to show my puppy to everyone," Solomon said as he and Sara headed for school the next day.

Sara nodded. "I'm glad Teacher Naomi said we could bring pets on the last day of school."

"*Jah* [Yes]," said Solomon. "Today should be lots of fun!"

When Solomon and Sara entered the school yard, he spotted several children gathered on the lawn, playing with their pets. There were goats, kittens, dogs, rabbits, chickens, ducks, and even a turtle.

Sara's friend Ellen rushed up to Solomon. "You're puppy's so cute. Can I hold her awhile?"

Solomon shook his head. "Peaches doesn't like anyone to hold her but me."

"That's *lecherich* [ridiculous]," Ellen said. "Puppies don't care who holds them. They just like to be petted." She held out her hands, but Solomon wouldn't budge.

"You're sure selfish," Solomon's friend John said. He nudged Ellen's arm. "Why don't you ask Willie if you can play with Sam, his floppy-eared dog?"

"I think I will!" Ellen said tearfully as she scampered away.

Solomon sat on the grass with the puppy in his lap. "Did you bring a pet with you today?" he asked John.

John shook his head. "I figured I'd get to play with your puppy, but I guess that's not going to happen."

John turned his back on Solomon. "I'd rather not talk to someone who's selfish and mean."

Solomon hung his head in shame.

A few weeks ago Sara had learned a lesson on selfishness, and now Solomon was doing the very same thing. He felt bad for hurting his friends.

Solomon hurried over to Ellen. "I was wrong for not letting you pet my puppy." He handed Peaches to her and smiled. "You can pet the puppy as much as you want."

"You can pet Peaches, too," Solomon said, turning to John.

"I don't want to be known as a selfish boy. I want to be known for my wisdom, good deeds, and kind words." Solomon pointed to himself. " 'Even a child is known by his actions.' "

Glossary

of Amish Words and Phrases

absatz—stop
ach—oh
baremlich—terrible
boppli—baby
bussli—kitten
daed—dad
danki—thanks
dumm—dumb
epplebei—apple pie
faul—lazy
gees—goats
grank—sick
jah—yes
kinner—children
lecherich—ridiculous
mamm—mom
nee—no
neggel—nails
oi—egg
schmaert—smart
schtrick—rope
seef—soap
siesses—sugar
wunderbaar—wonderful
Wie geht's?—How are you?